dear juno

by **Soyung Pak**

illustrated by **Susan Kathleen Hartung**

PUFFIN BOOKS

PUFFIN BOOKS
Published by Penguin Group
Penguin Young Readers Group, 345 Hudson Street, New York, New York 10014, U.S.A.
Penguin Books Ltd, 80 Strand, London WC2R 0RL, England
Penguin Books Australia Ltd, 250 Camberwell Road, Camberwell, Victoria 3124, Australia
Penguin Books Canada Ltd, 10 Alcorn Avenue, Toronto, Ontario, Canada M4V 3B2
Penguin Books (N.Z.) Ltd, 182-190 Wairau Road, Auckland 10, New Zealand

First published in the United States of America by Viking, a division of Penguin Putnam Books for Young Readers, 1999
Published by Puffin Books, a division of Penguin Putnam Books for Young Readers, 2001

7 9 10 8 6

Text copyright © Soyung Pak, 1999
Illustrations copyright © Susan Kathleen Hartung, 1999
All rights reserved

THE LIBRARY OF CONGRESS HAS CATALOGED THE VIKING EDITION AS FOLLOWS:
Pak, Soyung.
Dear Juno / by Soyung Pak; illustrated by Susan Kathleen Hartung.
p. cm.
Summary: Although Juno, a Korean American boy, cannot read the letter he receives from
his grandmother in Seoul, he understands what it means from the photograph and
dried flower that are enclosed and decides to send a similar letter to her.
ISBN 0-670-88252-6 (hc.)
[1. Grandmothers—Fiction. 2. Letters—Fiction. 3. Korean Americans—fiction.]
I. Hartung, Susan Kathleen, ill. II. Title.
PZ7.P173De 1999 [Fic]—dc21 98-43408 CIP AC

Puffin Books ISBN 0-14-230017-9

Printed in U.S.A.

The illustrations for this book were created using oil paint glazes on sealed paper.
The paint is blotted and manipulated to create different effects.

For my mother and father, with love
—S.P.

In loving memory of my grandma and my oma
—S.K.H.

juno watched as the red and white blinking lights soared across the night sky like shooting stars, and waited as they disappeared into faraway places. Juno wondered where they came from. He wondered where they were going. And he wondered if any of the planes came from a little town near Seoul where his grandmother lived, and where she ate persimmons every evening before bed.

Juno looked at the letter that came that day. It was long and white and smudged. He saw the red and blue marks on the edges and knew the letter came from far away. His name and address were neatly printed on the front, so he knew the letter was for him. But best of all, the special stamp on the corner told Juno that the letter was from his grandmother.

Through the window Juno could see his parents. He saw bubbles growing in the sink. He saw dirty dishes waiting to be washed. He knew he
would have to wait for the cleaning to be done before his parents could
read the letter to him.

"Maybe I can read the inside, too," Juno said to his dog, Sam. Sam wagged his tail. Very carefully, Juno opened the envelope. Inside, he found a letter folded into a neat, small square.

He unfolded it. Tucked inside were a picture and a dried flower.

Juno looked at the letters and words he couldn't understand. He pulled out the photograph. It was a picture of his grandmother holding a cat. He pulled out the red and yellow flower. It felt light and gentle like a dried leaf. Juno smiled. "C'mon, Sam," Juno said. "Let's find Mom and Dad."

"Grandma has a new cat," Juno said as he handed the letter to his mother. "And she's growing red and yellow flowers in her garden."

"How do you know she has a new cat?" Juno's father asked.

"She wouldn't send me a picture of a strange cat," said Juno.

"I guess not," said Juno's father.

"How do you know the flower is from her garden?" asked Juno's mother.

"She wouldn't send me a flower from someone else's garden," Juno answered.

"No, she wouldn't," said Juno's mother.

Then Juno's mother read him the letter.

Dear Juno,

    How are you? I have a new cat to keep me company. I named him Juno after you. He can't help me weed, but the rabbits no longer come to eat my flowers.

                               Grandma

    "Just like you read it yourself,"
Juno's father said.
    "I did read it," Juno said.
    "Yes, you did," said his mother.

At school, Juno showed his class his grandmother's picture and dried flower. His teacher even pinned the letter to the board. All day long, Juno kept peeking at the flower from his grandmother's garden. He didn't have a garden that grew flowers, but he had a swinging tree.

Juno looked at the letter pinned to the board. Did his grandmother like getting letters, too? Yes, Juno thought. She likes getting letters just like I do. So Juno decided to write one.

After school, Juno ran to his backyard. He picked a leaf from the swinging tree — the biggest leaf he could find.

Juno found his mother, who was sitting at her desk. He showed her the leaf. "I'm going to write a letter," he told her.

"I'm sure it will be a very nice letter," she answered, and gave him a big yellow envelope.

"Yes it will," Juno said, and then he began to draw.

First, he drew a picture of his mom and dad standing outside the house. Second, he drew a picture of Sam playing underneath his big swinging tree. Then very carefully, Juno drew a picture of himself standing under an airplane in a starry, nighttime sky. After he was finished, he placed everything in the envelope.

"Here's my letter," Juno announced proudly. "You can read it if you want."

Juno's father looked in the envelope.

He pulled out the leaf. "Only a big swinging tree could grow a leaf this big," he said.

Juno's mother pulled out one of the drawings. "What a fine picture," she said. "It takes a good artist to say so much with a drawing."

Juno's father patted Juno on the head. "It's just like a real letter," he said.

"It is a real letter," Juno said.

"It certainly is," said his mother. Then they mailed the envelope and waited.

One day a big envelope came. It was from Juno's grandmother. This time, Juno didn't wait at all. He opened the envelope right away.

Inside, Juno found a box of colored pencils. He knew she wanted another letter.

Next, he pulled out a picture of his grandmother. He noticed she was sitting with a cat and two kittens. He thought for a moment and laughed. Now his grandmother would have to find a new name for her cat—in Korea, Juno was a boy's name, not a girl's.

Then he pulled out a small toy plane.

Juno smiled. His grandmother was coming to visit.

"Maybe she'll bring her cat when she comes to visit," Juno said to Sam as he climbed into bed. "Maybe you two will be friends."

❄   ❄   ❄

Soon Juno was fast asleep. And when he dreamed that night, he dreamed about a faraway place, a village just outside Seoul, where his grandmother, whose gray hair sat on top of her head like a powdered doughnut, was sipping her morning tea.

The cool air feels crisp against her cheek. Crisp enough to crackle, he dreams, like the golden leaves which cover the persimmon garden.